CAPTAIN AWESOME

GOES TO SUPERHERO CAMP

By STAN KIRBY

Illustrated by GEORGE O'CONNOR

LITTLE SIMON

New York   London   Toronto   Sydney   New Delhi

 LITTLE SIMON

An imprint of Simon & Schuster Children's Publishing Division • 1230 Avenue of the Americas, New York, New York 10020 • First Little Simon paperback edition May 2015 • Copyright © 2015 by Simon & Schuster, Inc. All rights reserved, including the right of reproduction in whole or in part in any form. LITTLE SIMON is a registered trademark of Simon & Schuster, Inc., and associated colophon is a trademark of Simon & Schuster, Inc. For information about special discounts for bulk purchases, please contact Simon & Schuster Special Sales at 1-866-506-1949 or business@simonandschuster.com. The Simon & Schuster Speakers Bureau can bring authors to your live event. For more information or to book an event contact the Simon & Schuster Speakers Bureau at 1-866-248-3049 or visit our website at www.simonspeakers.com. Designed by Jay Colvin. The text of this book was set in Little Simon Gazette. Manufactured in the United States of America 0415 FFG

10 9 8 7 6 5 4 3 2 1

Library of Congress Cataloging-in-Publication Data

Kirby, Stan. Captain Awesome goes to superhero camp / by Stan Kirby ; illustrated by George O'Connor. — First edition. pages cm. — (Captain Awesome ; 14) Summary: "Captain Awesome and the Sunnyview Superhero Squad can't wait to venture into the woods and get some real superhero training at Camp Ka-Pow. That is, until they meet the Cloudy Heights Super Crew. These campers must be supervillains in disguise"— Provided by publisher. [1. Camps—Fiction. 2. Superheroes—Fiction. 3. Supervillains—Fiction.] I. O'Connor, George, illustrator. II. Title. PZ7.K633529Cagp 2015 [Fic]—dc23 2014021717

ISBN 978-1-4814-3154-5 (hc)

ISBN 978-1-4814-3153-8 (pbk)

ISBN 978-1-4814-3155-2 (eBook)

Table of Contents

CHAPTER 1

Boredom Patrol

By
Eugene

Give me a status update, team!" Captain Awesome called out from the head of the pack.

Captain Awesome, Supersonic Sal, and Nacho Cheese Man were pedaling their Cycles of Justice as fast as they could. They were on the lookout for danger.

"No alien invasion!" shouted Supersonic Sal.

"No vibrations from Mole Mandini and the Undergrounders!" Nacho Cheese Man yelled. "Whoa, stop sign!"

"I see it," Captain Awesome said. The heroes braked and looked both ways. "All clear," said their leader.

Morning patrol was what all great superheroes did. It was how Super Dude started every day. And Eugene McGillicudy was determined to follow his example.

That's right.

SUPER DUDE.

You've never heard of him? He's only the world's greatest super-hero. He once tucked the Sleepless Knight into a prison bed with his knockout punch. And another time he snapped the Ultimate Worrier's Sword of Complaint right in half!

Super Dude was the star of the Super Dude comic books that Eugene and his friends Charlie Thomas Jones and Sally Williams read whenever they were not watching *The Adventures of Super Dude* cartoons.

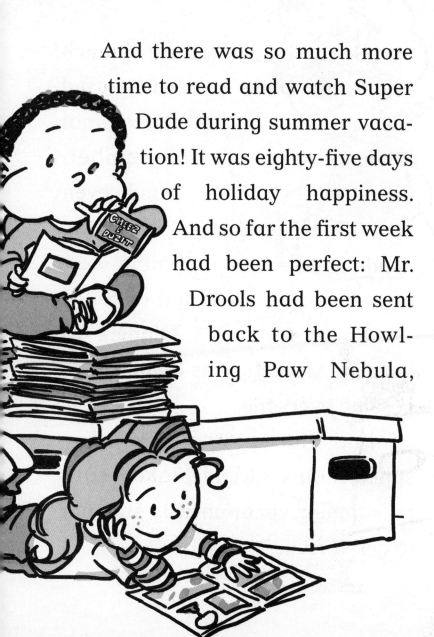

And there was so much more time to read and watch Super Dude during summer vacation! It was eighty-five days of holiday happiness. And so far the first week had been perfect: Mr. Drools had been sent back to the Howling Paw Nebula,

Dr. Yuck Spinach was chased out of town until September, and even Queen Stinkypants had a new brand of Solar Diapers to keep her Galactic Gas Bombs from gassing everyone.

But with most of the many supervillains already taken care of, summer vacation was starting to get boring.

If only there was something to do, Eugene thought.

FLASH!

What was that? Captain Awesome's Awesome-Sense began to tingle.

Captain Awesome turned to look. Suddenly, he was blasted by dozens of bright pink sparkles. "Sparkle bomb!" he yelled as his bike hit the curb.

PLOP!

Captain Awesome landed on the ground right in front of his arch-nemesis: Meredith Mooney.

"Little Miss Stinky Pinky!" Captain Awesome cried. Meredith

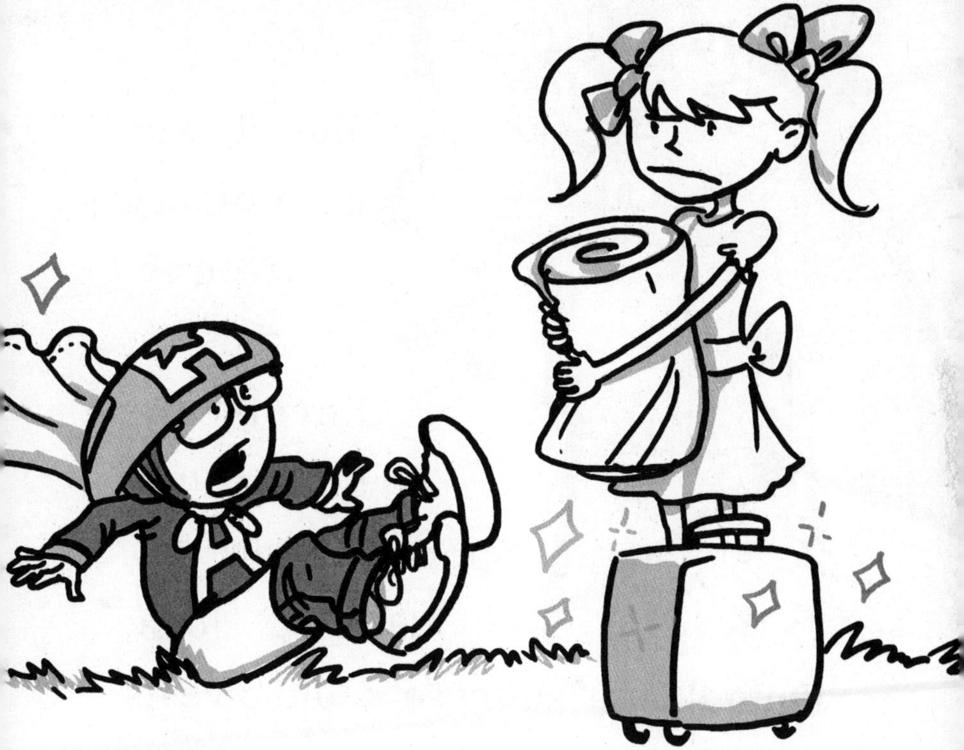

was standing in front of her family's van. She had a bright-pink sleeping bag rolled up in her evil clutches. A sparkly pink suitcase was at her side.

But it was no ordinary suitcase. It was a Level-Four Stinky Pink Sparkle Laser!

"Don't look, Squad! That 'suitcase' could give us *pink* eye and blind us forever!"

"I don't have time for this, Puke-Gene," Meredith said. "I'm going to the Sparkle Princess Camp-a-Thon." She stuffed her sleeping bag into the backseat and climbed in next to it. "It's girls only, so you're not allowed!" she said. "Smell you later!" With that, she slammed the door, stuck out her tongue, and pressed it against the window. She looked like a pink flesh-eating suckerfish.

CHAPTER 2

Ka-Pow!

BY
Eugene

All quiet in the neighborhood, Mom," Eugene said when he got home. "Too quiet! We've already defeated all the villains in Sunnyview, and ever since school got out, not one single bad guy has tried to take over the town."

"Surely, something fun . . . I mean, *bad*, must have happened this morning," Mrs. McGillicudy said.

"Well, I did see Meredith,"

Eugene replied. "That was pretty evil. But even she's leaving town for summer camp. Gross-me-out girly *princess* summer camp!"

"Camp sounds like fun," Mrs. McGillicudy said.

"Yeah, but not girly *princess*

camp!" Eugene said. "There should be crime-fighting tips and gadget labs to make your own gear and lessons on how to be invisible."

"It *would* be nice if there was a place just like that," Mrs. McGillicudy agreed.

"Nice? It would be awesome!"

Eugene said. "Heroes from all over would gather. It would be the ulti-mate team-up of the Hero League Society and the Society League of Heroes!"

"Hmm. I wonder if there is a summer camp like that," his mom said thoughtfully.

Eugene slowly shook his head. "Probably not," he said. "But a kid can dream."

That evening Eugene slumped toward the dinner table. He was still bored. Just as he was about to sit down . . .

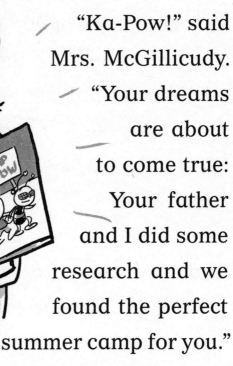

"Ka-Pow!" said Mrs. McGillicudy. "Your dreams are about to come true: Your father and I did some research and we found the perfect summer camp for you." She held out a brochure. "Surprise!"

Eugene scanned the piece of bright-blue paper. "'Camp Ka-pow: fifty acres of superhero training for heroic boys and girls," he recited.

Suddenly Eugene's eyes lit up like fireballs. "I've got to tell Charlie and Sally! Can they come too?"

"I've already spoken to their parents. Everything is all set for tomorrow," Mrs. McGillicudy said.

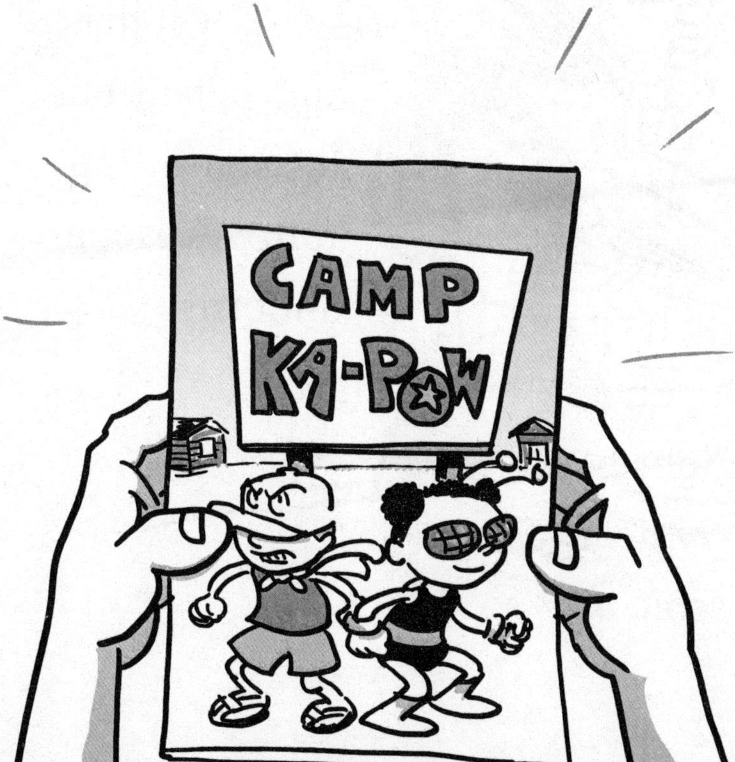
CAMP
KA-POW

TOMORROW?!

Eugene couldn't wait for dinner to end. He had to start packing! As soon as he finished the last evil pea on his plate, he raced up to his room, opened the secret drawer in his For-tress of Clothes, and pulled out his spare Captain Awesome uniform.

Camp Ka-Pow was Eugene's chance. It would be his opportunity to learn every skill it took to be the MI-TEEest superhero ever.

Once he was packed and ready for bed, Eugene lay back on his pillow. What would he learn first? Would it be "Sidekicks: Your Best Friend!" or "How to Pick the Perfect Secret Identity!" or maybe "Costume Repair When Your Mom Isn't Around"?

Eugene smiled and closed his eyes. Camp Ka-Pow was going to be the best camp ever!

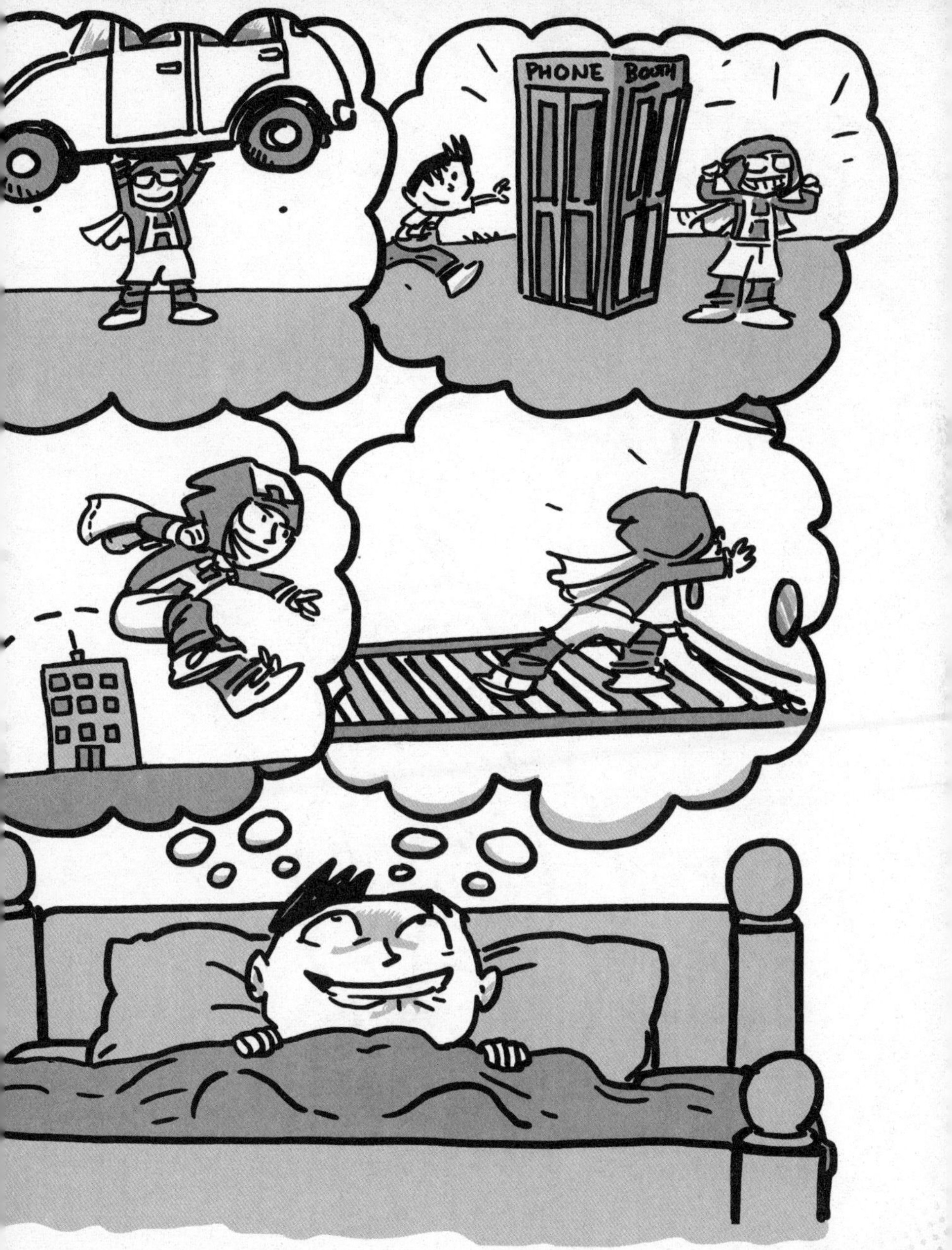
PHONE BOOTH

CHAPTER 3

Base Camp

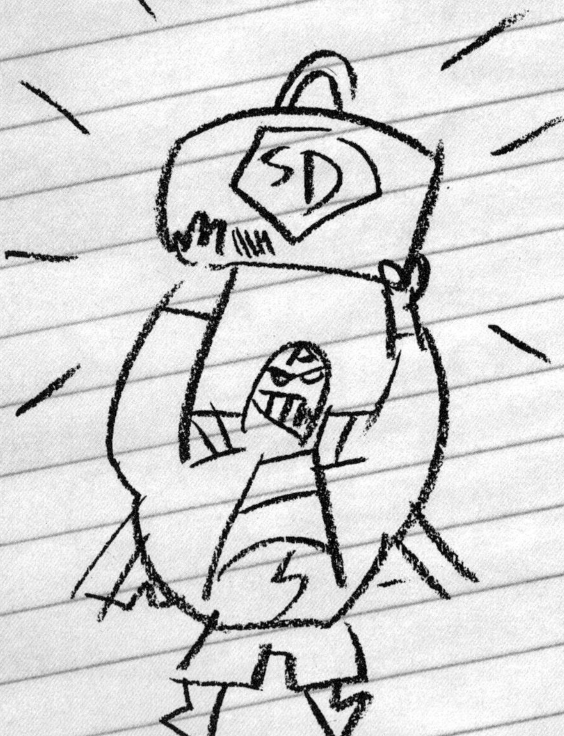

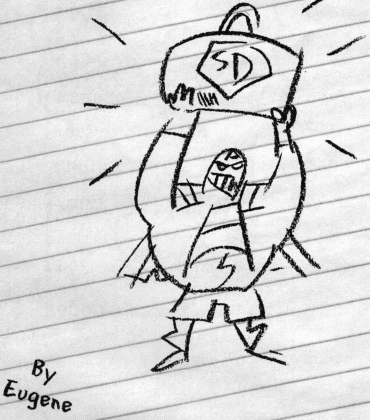

By Eugene

A voice boomed over the loudspeaker: "Welcome to Camp Ka-Pow!"

The doors of several yellow buses hissed open. "Yay!" dozens of kids shouted with glee. Some were already wearing capes and masks as they poured out into the camp's parking lot.

Eugene, Charlie, and Sally stepped off their bus. The wooden

archway held a banner that read WELCOME HEROES. It was decorated with bright orange lightning bolts.

"We're here!" Charlie shouted.

"This is already awesome!" Eugene cried.

"When can we learn how to fight evil better?" Sally asked.

"Whoa-ho-ho, little heroes! Not so fast!" A teenager stood at the entrance to the camp, holding a clipboard. He was dressed in a yellow mask and a yellow jumpsuit with black stripes. He had matching yellow boots, and he was wearing a whistle around his neck.

"I'm Super Todd, one of the many mighty counselors here at Camp Ka-Pow. Grab your bags, and we'll head over to the Ka-Power Theater for a heroes' welcome."

All the bags were stacked out-side the entrance. Eugene, Charlie, and Sally went over to pick them up.

"Stop!" Eugene cried out. "Bag thief!"

Eugene ran to the bags. His Super
Dude duffel bag was slung around
the shoulder of another camper.

The boy carrying the duffel
turned to face Eugene. "What's your
problem, dude?"

"That's my Super Dude bag," Eugene said. "I can tell because mine has a jelly stain on the side."

"That's not jelly," the boy replied. "That's grape juice. *My* grape juice."

Eugene put his hand on one of the straps and held tight. "No, it's *my* jelly."

The boy pulled the duffel toward himself. "My juice!"

The two boys pulled the bag back and forth. "My jelly! My juice! My jelly! My juice!" they said to each other.

I may have to use Captain Awesome's Mi-Tee power, Eugene thought.

"Found it, Eric!" A smaller boy ran down the sidewalk toward the great Baggage Battle. He held up a Super Dude duffel bag. "I recognized the juice stain."

Suddenly, the boy, Eric, let go of Eugene's bag, and Eugene went flying! Eric didn't even say sorry as he walked away.

"Let's go, Eugene," Sally said. They threw their bags over their shoulders and followed Super Todd and the other heroes in to the small amphitheater. Eugene kept his eye on Eric until they sat down on the wooden benches that surrounded the stage.

CHAPTER 4

Camp Rules!

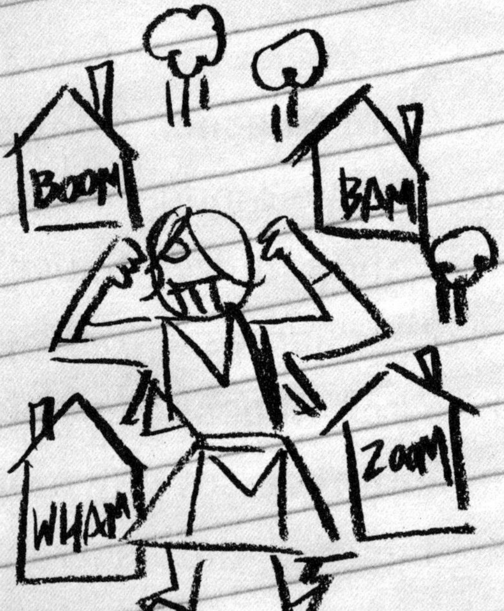
BOOM
BAM
WHAM
ZOOM

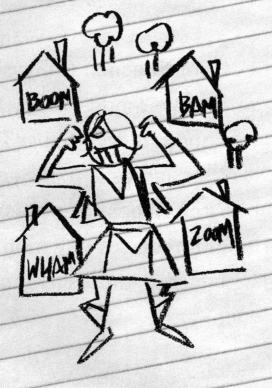

By
Eugene

Drums started to beat. Music *thump-thump-thump*ed. Smoke filled the stage. There was excitement in the air. No one was talking.

Then from out of the smoke stepped Super Todd. "Welcome, heroes!" he said. Everyone in the audience cheered. "In the life of a superhero there are three things you never forget: you never forget your first crime-fighting adventure. . . ."

Eugene knew that was true!

"You never forget
the friends who
help you in your
time of need."

Eugene,
Charlie, and Sally
looked at one another
and smiled. That was definitely true.

"And you'll never forget your time here at CAMP KA-POW!" he yelled.

The crowd of superheroes roared with excitement.

According to Super Todd, Camp Ka-Pow was fifty acres of prime superhero adventure. There were woods off to the north end of camp where the Tree House of Destiny

lurked. Next to it was
the Superhero Flight School, and
at the edge of the woods was Lake
Justice, "with a dock for any of you
with special water powers," Super
Todd said. There were also climbing walls, obstacle courses, ropes to
swing on, and so much more.

"Now let's meet some of
my super team!" Super
Todd said.

Commander
Chef stepped
onstage wear-
ing a red-white-

and-blue apron and a star-studded
chef's hat."Breakfast is every morning at seven a.m.," Commander
Chef said. There were groans from
some of the campers, especially

the kid dressed as a bat. "The Bat Knight doth not approveth of such early hours," the kid complained.

Then Mary Marvelous said there were three main rules at camp:

(1) No littering. Keep the camp clean because a messy camp is like inviting evil to a party.

(2) Obey the curfew. It's "Lights-out!" at eight p.m., and everyone has to be in their cabins. Night patrol will be handled by the Camp Ka-Pow Super Patrol Team.

And finally a rule that was actually pretty awesome:

(3) Team up! Camp Ka-Pow is all about teamwork and learning to work together.

After the announcements, the young heroes formed a line by the stage. Super Todd held up a list

and started calling out names and cabins.

"Jim! You're in cabin BOOM! Laura, WHAM! Samantha, BAM!"

Charlie and Eugene were given ZOOM! Sally got BAM!

"All right, campers. Head to your cabins!" Mary Marvelous shouted.

CHAPTER 5

Bunk-Bed Bandits

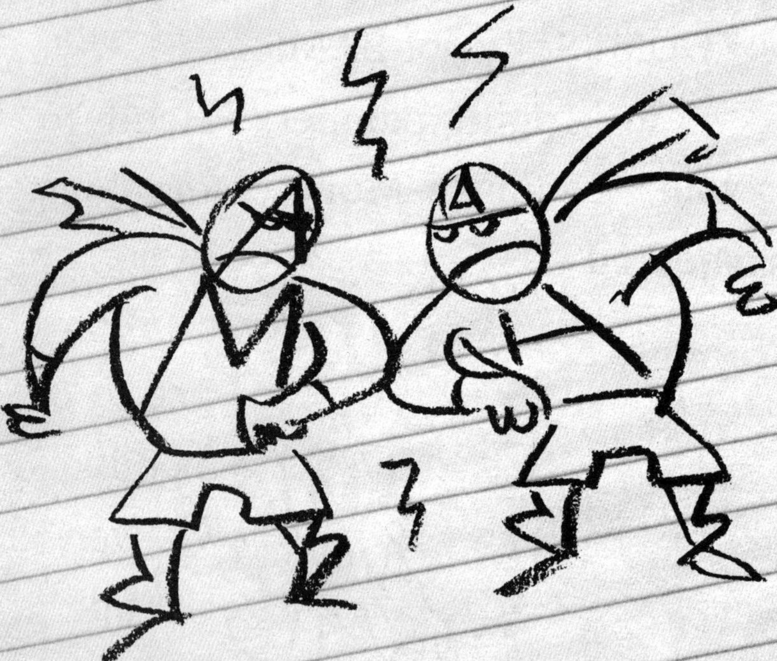

By
Eugene

Eugene and Charlie stood in the doorway of ZOOM! the cabin that had been assigned to them. "Wow," they said.

It was decorated like a super-hero's headquarters. The bathroom door looked like the entrance to a secret lair, the rug was shaped like a rocket, and the windows were round like the portholes on Super Admiral's Flying Fortress.

But most important, there were bunk beds against the wall.

BUNK BEDS!

"I've always wanted to sleep on a top bunk!" Eugene said. He and Charlie both smiled and high-fived. Just as their palms slapped, two boys rushed in.

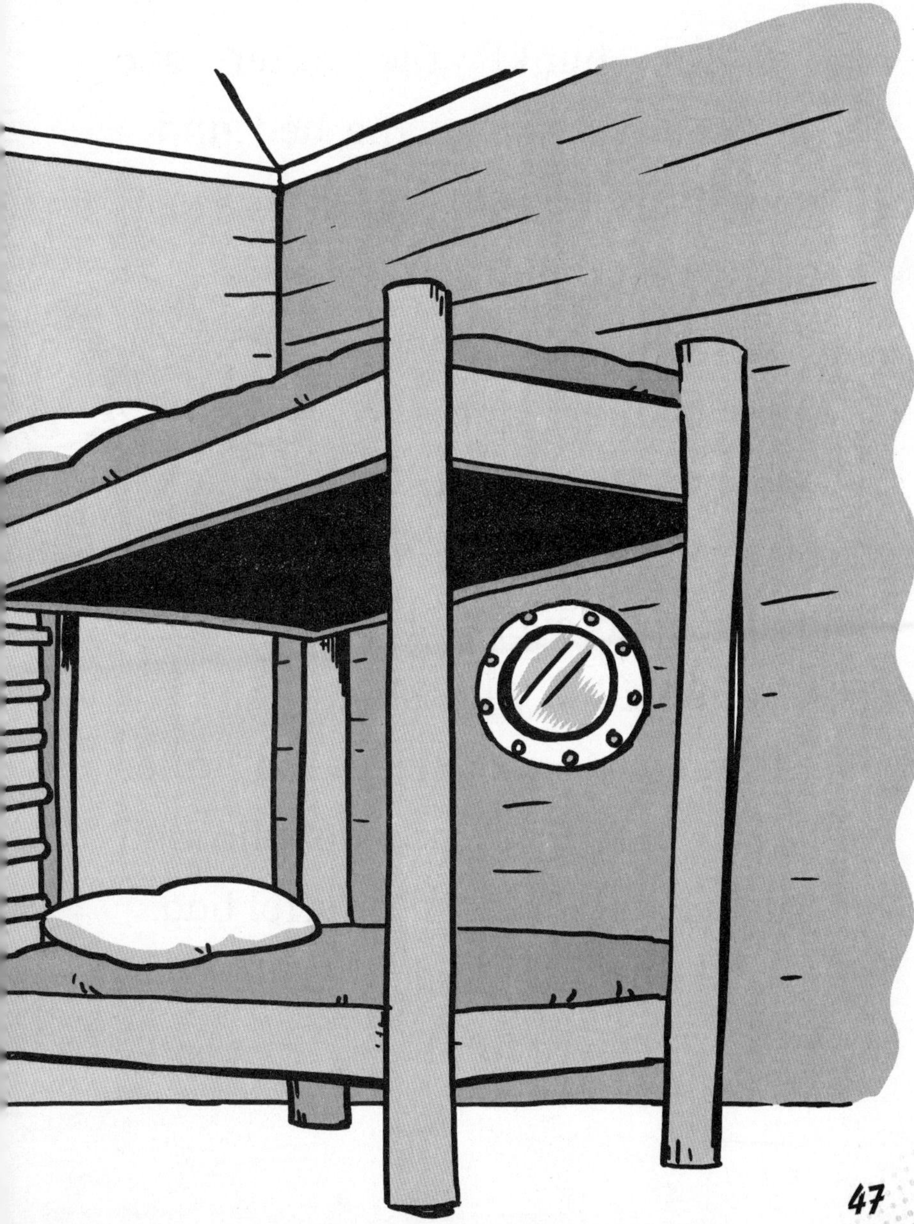

"Top bunk!" the taller one shouted. He ran to the bed and tossed his bag on top of the first bunk.

"Other top bunk!" the smaller one shouted. He climbed on to the first top bunk and leaped over to the second with a whoosh.

Eugene recognized the taller boy. It was Eric, the one who had tried to steal Eugene's duffel bag.

"Hey, guys!" Eugene called out. "We were here first!"

"Yeah, we should get the top
bunks," Charlie said.

"No way. We called it from the
bus in the parking lot," Eric said.
"Right, Chris?"

"Yep! We win!" Chris cheered.

Eugene and Charlie deflated.

Super Todd popped his head in the doorway. "You guys are needed outside in five minutes," he said. "We're going on our first mission."

He disappeared, closing the door behind him. A moment later the door opened again. "Oh, and you might want to gear up," he said with a wink. "This is superhero camp!"

"To the costumes!" Eugene

grabbed his clothes and headed to the bathroom to change. *It's better if people don't know I'm Captain Awesome yet,* he thought.

BAGS!
UNZIP!
CAPE!
SUPERHEROES!

"We're going to have to keep an eye on Chris and Eric," Captain Awesome whispered to Nacho Cheese Man as he tied his cape. "First he tried to steal my

Super Dude duffel bag, and now he's stolen our beds. We might be bunking with secret bad guys."

"I'll bring my extra cheese,"
Nacho Cheese Man said. "Evil
hates cheese in a can."

CHAPTER 6

The Breakers of Ice!

By
Eugene

Captain Awesome and Nacho Cheese Man followed Super Todd past the Hero Recharging Station and the Commander General Store, which sold the latest crime-fighting gadgets. Then they turned left at the Crime Fighters' Cafeteria, crossed the Lava Bridge, and went into a clearing, where several other heroes were already waiting.

"Eug—I mean, Captain Awesome!

Over here!" Supersonic Sal called.

Captain Awesome and Nacho
Cheese Man sat next to her. "Wait
until you hear who stole our beds!"
Captain Awesome said. But he was
interrupted by Super Todd.

"Okay, time for icebreakers!"
Super Todd said.

"Ready!" said Captain Awesome.

"Should we break the ice with Fists of Awesome Fury or Feet of Shoeless Force?" he asked.

Super Todd laughed. "Icebreakers is when we tell one another a little about ourselves and our powers." He pointed to Captain Awesome. "How about you go first?"

Eugene sat up straight. "I'm Captain Awesome. My friends and I are the three members of the

Sunnyview Superhero Squad," he said as he pointed to Supersonic Sal and Nacho Cheese Man. "I have the MI-TEE powers of awesomeness," he declared in his most heroic voice ever.

"Awesomeness? That's not even a word!" Even with the speaker's face hidden by a mask, Captain

Awesome recognized the voice immediately.

ERIC.

The bunk-bed thief!

"*I'm* Amazing Man," the masked boy continued. "I have Amazing Power and every time I use it, people come for miles around just to say, 'That hero is amazing!'"

"It's true," said the boy next to Amaz-ing Man. He had glasses and a purple shirt and wore a bicycle helmet that looked like a giant pink brain. "I'm Whiz Kid, and I have the brain power of *ten* kids," he declared.

Whiz Kid pointed to the girl sitting next to Supersonic Sal. "And this is Super Silent Sam," he said. "She's quieter than the quietest mouse. You wouldn't want her to sneak up on you."

"We're the proud crew members of the Cloudy Heights Super Crew!" Amazing Man said.

"Cloudy Heights! Cloudy Heights! No evil shall escape our sights!" Amazing Man and Whiz Kid chanted.

The others in the group intro-
duced themselves and their powers. There was Bat Knight, who
had the power to hang upside
down without getting dizzy; Cartoon Carl, who could imitate any
cartoon character; Sneaky Petra,
who had spy powers; and Wanda

Wonderful, a magician who pulled a quarter from behind Nacho Cheese Man's ear.

Once everyone had finished, Super Todd stood up and said, "It's time for our first challenge. This will test the skills of all superheroes. We're headed to the Laser Beam Training Course!"

Every superhero in the group gasped with excitement.

GASP!

"Laser Beam Training!" Captain Awesome said. He looked at Supersonic Sal and Nacho Cheese Man. "This place just keeps getting better and better!"

CHAPTER 7

ZZZAPPED!

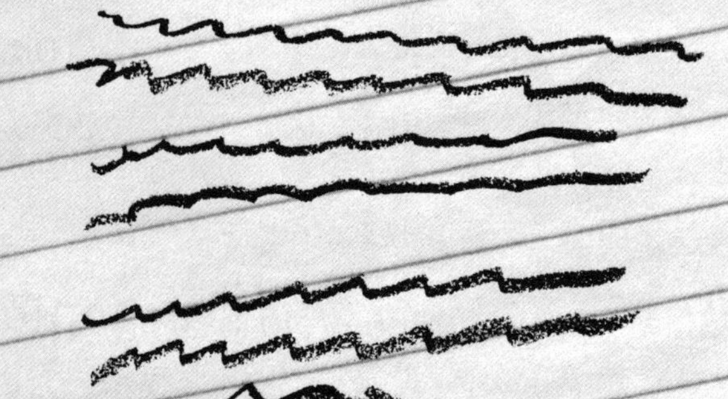

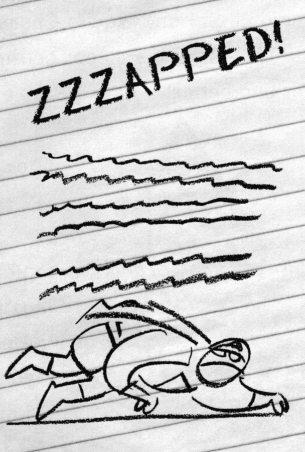

By
Eugene

The heroes lined up in front of two rock climbing walls. Orange yarn crisscrossed the space between the two walls like a crazy plate of spaghetti.

"Welcome to Lasertopia!" said Super Todd. "About a bazillion orange lasers are shooting between those walls to test your speed and balance. Your mission," Super Todd continued, "is to get to the other side without touching a single beam. So, who wants to go first?"

Supersonic Sal stepped forward. "I'll go!"

ROLL!
DIVE!
TWIST!

Not even orange yarn lasers shooting at the speed of light could catch Supersonic Sal! She made it

through without touching a single one!

"Mi-Tee!" Captain Awesome cheered as Supersonic Sal waved to him from the far side.

Whiz Kid went next. He strolled up to the first row of

crisscrossing lasers and gave a big yawn.

"Child's play," he muttered. "My Super Duper Brain can easily calculate the safest course through the lasers using simple geometry."

Whiz Kid gave the Cloudy Heights Super Crew Salute. Then, with the grace of a ballet dancer and the speed of a turtle, Whiz Kid successfully made it through the lasers.

"Balance *that* equation!" he yelled back to the kids still on the other side.

"Awesome job, you two!" said Super Todd. "Okay, who wants to dare the Walls of Laser Zappiness next?"

Captain Awesome stepped forward. "I'll send those lasers back to the evil ball of yarn that they unrolled from!"

"May the Cheese be with you," said Nacho Cheese Man.

It's time to show those Cloudy Heights Super Goofs who the real superhero is! Captain Awesome thought as he charged for the lasers with a shout of "MI-TEEEEE!"

**JUMP!
ROLL!
TWIST!
TWANG!**

Twang?! Captain Awesome's foot was caught in a yarn laser. The more he struggled to break free, the more he tangled himself. Soon his whole body was wrapped up in yarn like a cape-wearing fly in a spider's knitted web.

"Aaaargh! I've been yarned!" Captain Awesome shouted. "Go! Complete the mission without me!"

As Nacho Cheese Man and Supersonic Sal rushed to help untangle Captain Awesome from the yarn, the rest of the heroes burst out in laughter.

And no one laughed louder than Amazing Man.

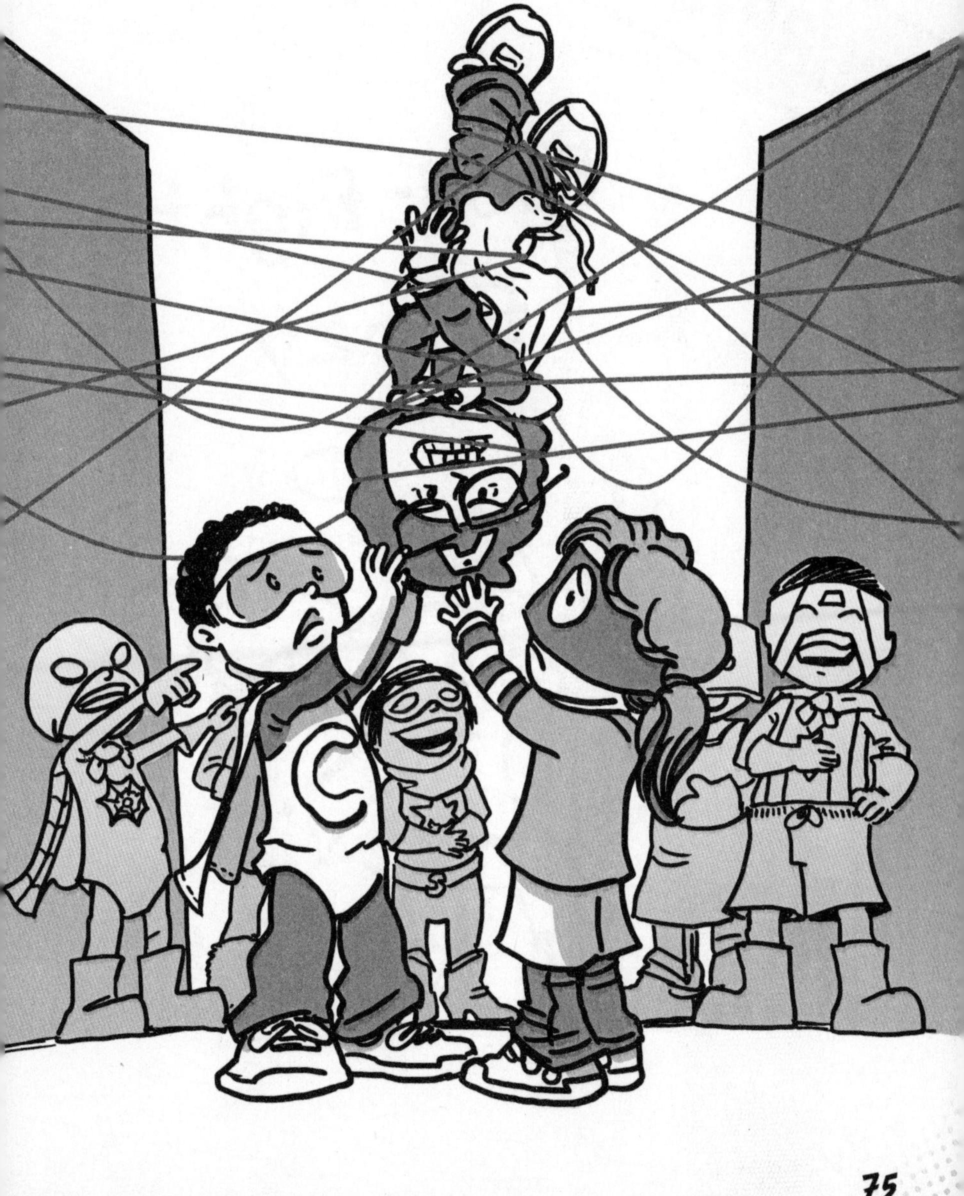

CHAPTER 8

Food-Fight Frenzy

By
Eugene

I'm telling you, the Cloudy Heights Super Crew should really be called the Cloudy Heights Super Crew of *Bad Guys!*" Captain Awesome whispered to Nacho Cheese Man and Supersonic Sal as they stood in line to get their dinner.

"Are you sure? Samantha has been nice enough to me," replied Supersonic Sal.

The trio of heroes took their

trays and headed toward six empty seats. But then the *worst* thing happened: Amazing Man, Whiz Kid, and Super Silent Sam slid into three of the open chairs.

"We can't sit next to *them* while we eat!" Captain Awesome gasped.

"Guys, I promise, Super Silent Sam isn't that bad," Supersonic Sal said. "Look. She's even smiling at us."

Super Silent Sam offered a small smile, then quietly took a bite of her hot dog.

"*Fine*, we'll sit next to them." Captain Awesome sighed. "But only because the other open seats are next to Stink Bomb Kid. He smells worse than Queen Stinkypants."

Captain Awesome and Amazing Man didn't take their eyes off each other as the Sunnyview Superhero Squad sat in the empty seats.

"By the way, Amazing Man, I did some measurements," Whiz Kid reported. "Dart is now 36.2 inches long from head to tail."

"Whoa! He's twice as big as last summer!" Amazing Man replied, breaking off his staring contest with Captain Awesome.

"Who's Dart?" Supersonic Sal asked.

"Only the most amazing side-kick in the history of sidekicks," Amazing Man declared. He pointed to a large iguana in a tank next to the window. "Dart stays at camp during the year and uses his super zap-tongue to keep the grounds safe from evil while we're away."

"Well, *my* sidekick is Turbo the hamster," Captain Awesome said.

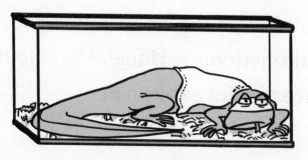

"And he could run circles around your bug zapper."

Just then, Nacho Cheese Man pressed the nozzle on his tri-flavored cheese. The can sputtered and spit out a glob of cheese that splattered on Whiz Kid's sleeve.

"Hey! Watch where you're pointing that thing! I'm lactose intolerant!" Whiz Kid snapped.

"Sorry! It was a major cheese malfunction. Honest!" Nacho Cheese Man explained.

"No one cheeses the Cloudy Heights Super Crew!" Amazing Man cried. He flung a spoonful of gooey mac and cheese at Nacho Cheese Man.

"And no one *mac*-and-cheeses the Sunnyview Superhero Squad!" Captain Awesome flung a spoonful of mashed potatoes. They splattered across Amazing Man's chest . . . *and* all over the back of a kid who called himself Captain Laser Eye.

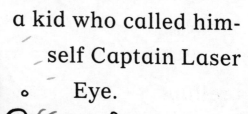

"Surprise Spud Sneak Attack!" Captain Laser Eye shouted, and threw a blob of mashed potatoes back at Captain Awesome.

Shouts of "food fight!" filled the air. Mashed potatoes, mac and cheese, pudding, hot dogs, peas, carrots . . . if it could be thrown, it

was soon sailing across the dining hall in a crazy explosion of food-fighting frenzy!

CHAPTER 9

Knot Heroic

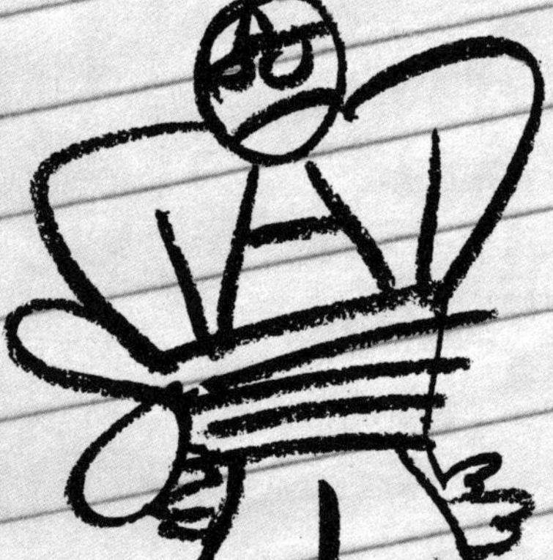

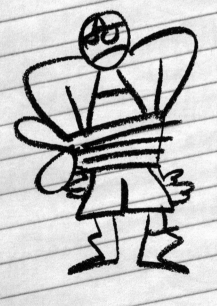

By
Eugene

Eugene learned two very important lessons that night. Lesson one: mac and cheese is great for dinner but *not* great to wear as a hat. Lesson two: food fights are awesome, but cleaning up after a food fight is the exact opposite.

Mary Marvelous gave a stern warning that messy food fights were for villains. And villains never get dessert. After that announcement,

none of the campers were happy
with Eugene or Eric.

The next day training started with
lessons on how to capture a supervillain.

"The first step is to make sure
the bad guys are always secure and

won't be able to escape. So I'm going to teach you how to make super-handcuffs." Super Todd held up a piece of blue rope. "This is unbreakable rope from Planet Rope-a-Ton!" he said.

"Oooh! I love alien rope!" Nacho Cheese Man said.

After learning to tie an Ultra Knotastical Knot, the heroes used their skills to capture a supervillain—who looked a lot like a scarecrow with a cape.

TWIRL!
THROW!
GOTCHA!

Captain Awesome easily lassoed the scarecrow.

As the other supercampers gave it a try, Captain Awesome leaned toward Nacho Cheese Man and Supersonic Sal. "Let's make

this a little harder. I bet I can capture a moving target!" he said.

"Okay. Try to catch me!" said
Supersonic Sal.

Captain Awesome twirled the
rope over his head. With a shout of
"Lasso away!" he
threw the loop right
at Supersonic Sal.
But Captain
Awesome
threw it
too hard. It went
over Sal's head
and lassoed

Amazing Man by mistake.

"Help! The scarecrow's got me!" Amazing Man yelled out, startled. Then he realized that the creepy scarecrow wasn't the one holding the other end of the rope.

"Oops," Captain Awesome said.

As Whiz Kid and Super Silent Sam rushed to help free him, Amazing Man glared at Captain Awesome. The rest of the kids burst into laughter at the accident.

The rest of the day was packed with classes in heroic speech-making, lessons on how to escape a supervillain's deathtrap, battle training with cardboard "robots,"

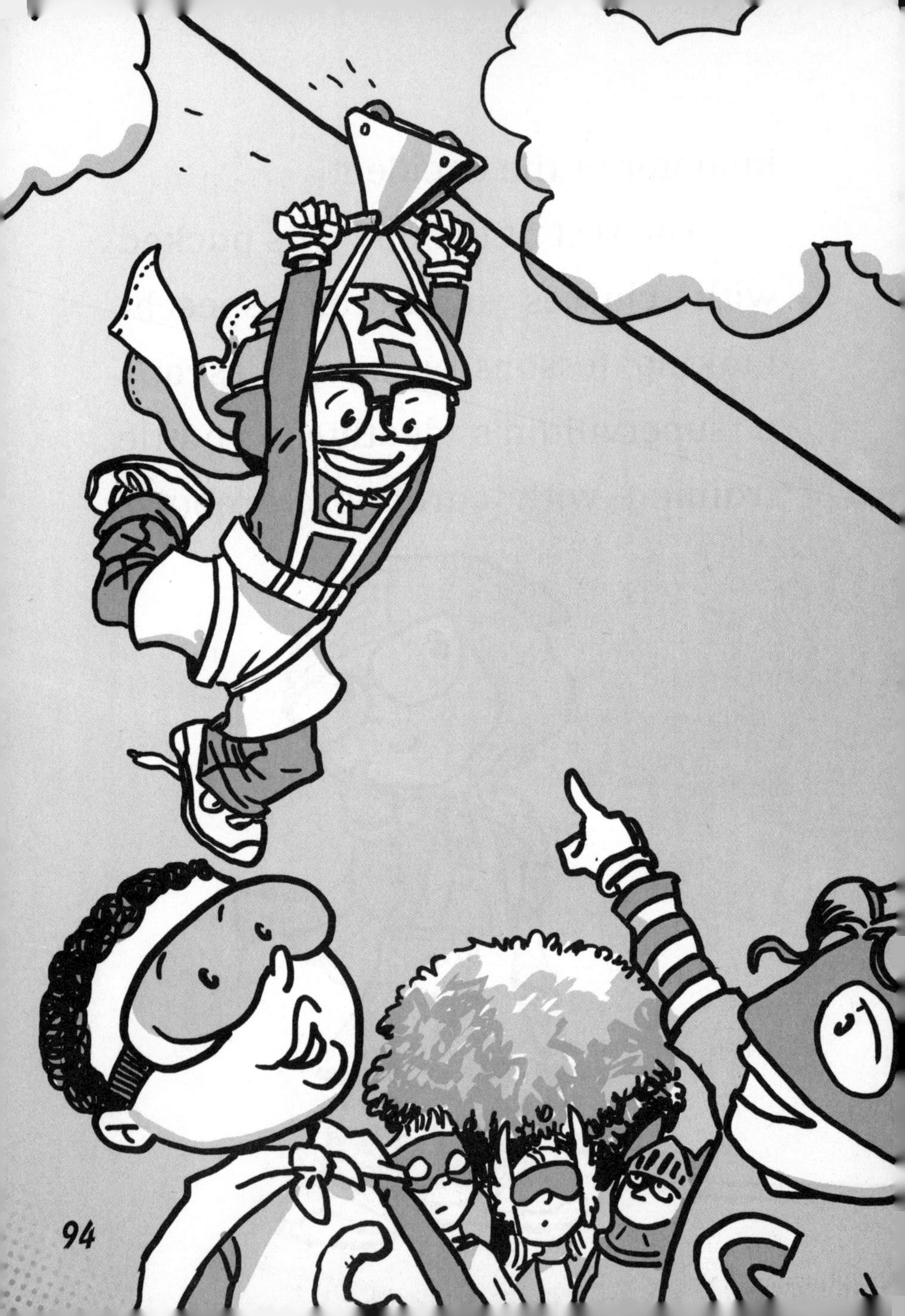

and flying high with flight training on the zip line.

Flying would be the best super-power ever! Eugene decided as he flew through the air.

CHAPTER 10

Superhero Team-Up

By
Eugene

Eugene and Charlie returned to their cabin and flopped onto their lame bottom bunks. "Oh man, what a day," said an exhausted Eugene. "Who knew training to save the world would be so tiring?"

"I'd like a supernap," Charlie agreed.

But just as Charlie's head hit the pillow, Super Todd raced into their cabin.

"Mary Marvelous has been cap-
tured by the supervillain
group the Evil Bunch!"
Super Todd cried. "We
need everyone's help
to rescue her!"

ZIP!
CAPE!
COSTUME!

Captain Awesome
and Nacho Cheese Man were ready
in a flash. They joined Super Todd
and the other heroes outside the
cabins.

Super Todd unrolled a map on

the ground. Mary Marvelous was being held at the far end of camp.

"Your mission is to save Mary Marvelous and make sure the Evil Bunch doesn't capture the Justice Cape." Super Todd pointed to a cape hanging from a nearby tree. "That

cape must not fall into the wrong hands!

"I gotta warn you though: These are some real nasty villains. They drink straight from the milk carton and they *never* share their desserts! Anyone who gets tagged by a supervillain is frozen until another hero tags them!" Super Todd said. He paused and looked directly at Captain Awesome before going on.

"The only way you'll be able to succeed in this mission is if you all work *together*." And with that, Super Todd blew his whistle and shouted, "Let's go!"

The supercampers charged like kids racing toward a birthday cake. One by one they were tagged by supervillains. Bat Knight! Frozen! Sneaky Petra! Frozen! Cartoon Carlton! Frozen! Stink Bomb Kid! Frozen—and still stinky! Frozen

Gal! Double frozen!

This isn't working! Captain Awesome realized as he watched hero after hero getting tagged. And no one had stayed behind to watch the Justice Cape!

Then the answer hit him like a pancake. This was just like the time Super Dude had to defeat Dr. Dentist and stop his Mighty Molar Army from drilling to the center of the Earth in Super Dude No. 111.

Super Dude had to team up with his archnemesis, Captain Copy Cat, who was basically a less cool copy of Super Dude.

"Two rights can never make a wrong, and heroes fighting together will be twice as strong!" It was what Super Dude had said as he and Captain Copy Cat flossed Dr. Dentist all the way to Tooth-catraz prison.

Captain Awesome skidded to a stop . . . which caused Amazing Man to collide with him and fall to the ground.

"You did that on purpose!" Amazing Man yelled.

Captain Awesome extended his hand. "'Two rights can never make a wrong, and heroes fighting together will be twice as strong.' If you join your amazingness with my awesomeness, no villains will be able to stop us."

Amazing Man looked up, surprised. "That's what Super Dude said when he teamed up with Captain Copy Cat in Super Dude No. 111. Together they kicked the cavity out of Dr. Dentist!"

TEAM UP!

Captain Awesome grabbed Amazing Man's hand and pulled him up. With the duel cry of "Mi-Teeee!"

and "Amaaaaaazing!" the greatest superhero superteam in the history of Camp Ka-Pow was formed!

CHAPTER II

Amazingly Awesome!

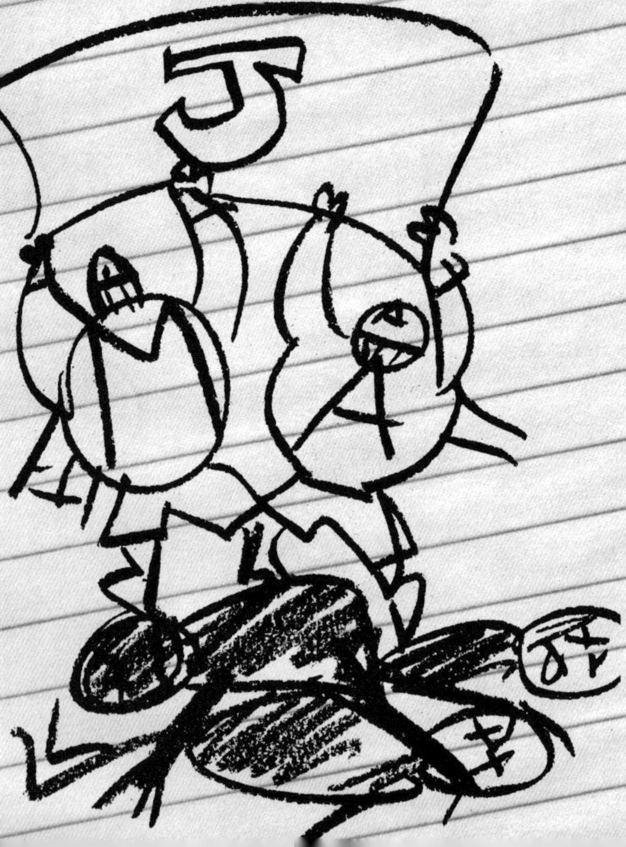

By Eugene

Okay, so here's the plan," Captain Awesome said. "Nacho Cheese Man: You use your canned cheese powers to distract the bad guys. Super Silent Sam, you sneak around as silently as you can and untag the frozen heroes. Supersonic Sal, since you're the fastest, it's up to you to save Mary Marvelous. And, Whiz Kid, use all your brainpower to figure out the safest path for Supersonic Sal to take to rescue her."

"And Captain Awesome and I will defend the Justice Cape," Amazing Man added. "There's no way any supervillains can get past us if we work together."

"Sunnyview Cloudy Heights Superhero Mega Crew, go!" the heroes chanted, and raced off on their separate missions.

Nacho Cheese Man sped past the villains, squirting cheese in the air. "Beware the power of canned cheese!" he shouted.

As the villains ran after him, Super Silent Sam quietly untagged

the frozen heroes. Meanwhile, Whiz Kid calculated the safest path to the captive Mary Marvelous. Supersonic Sal raced off like a rocket while Captain Awesome and Amazing Man guarded the Justice Cape.

When the villains realized Nacho Cheese Man was just a distraction, they charged for the cape.

TAG!
DODGE!
FREEZE!
DODGE!

Captain Awesome and Amazing Man used their amazingly awesome powers to freeze tag the villains and dodge being frozen themselves.

But then, just when it looked like they'd frozen every last villain, one reached for Amazing Man.

"Nooooooo!" Captain Awesome shouted, and dove right between Amazing Man and the villain.

TAG!

Captain Awesome fell to the ground, frozen. Amazing Man tagged the villain, freezing her too.

"You . . . you sacrificed your-self to save me?" Amazing Man asked.

"I did what any hero would do," Captain Awesome replied. "After all, good beating bad is what matters most."

"There's no superhero more Mi-Tee than you," Amazing Man said.

"Thanks. Now could you untag me so I can move?" requested Captain Awesome.

Amazing Man untagged Captain Awesome just as Supersonic Sal returned with Mary Marvelous.

The mission was over! The super-campers had won! "Three cheers for Captain Awesome!" Super Silent Sam called out.

Everyone stared at Super Silent Sam in stunned silence.

"What? He deserves it," she said.

The supercampers cheered: "Hip-hip-hooray! Hip-hip-hooray! Hip-hip-hooray!"

Nacho Cheese Man, Supersonic

Sal, Amazing Man, Whiz Kid, and Super Silent Sam high-fived! They had worked together as a team and defeated evil!

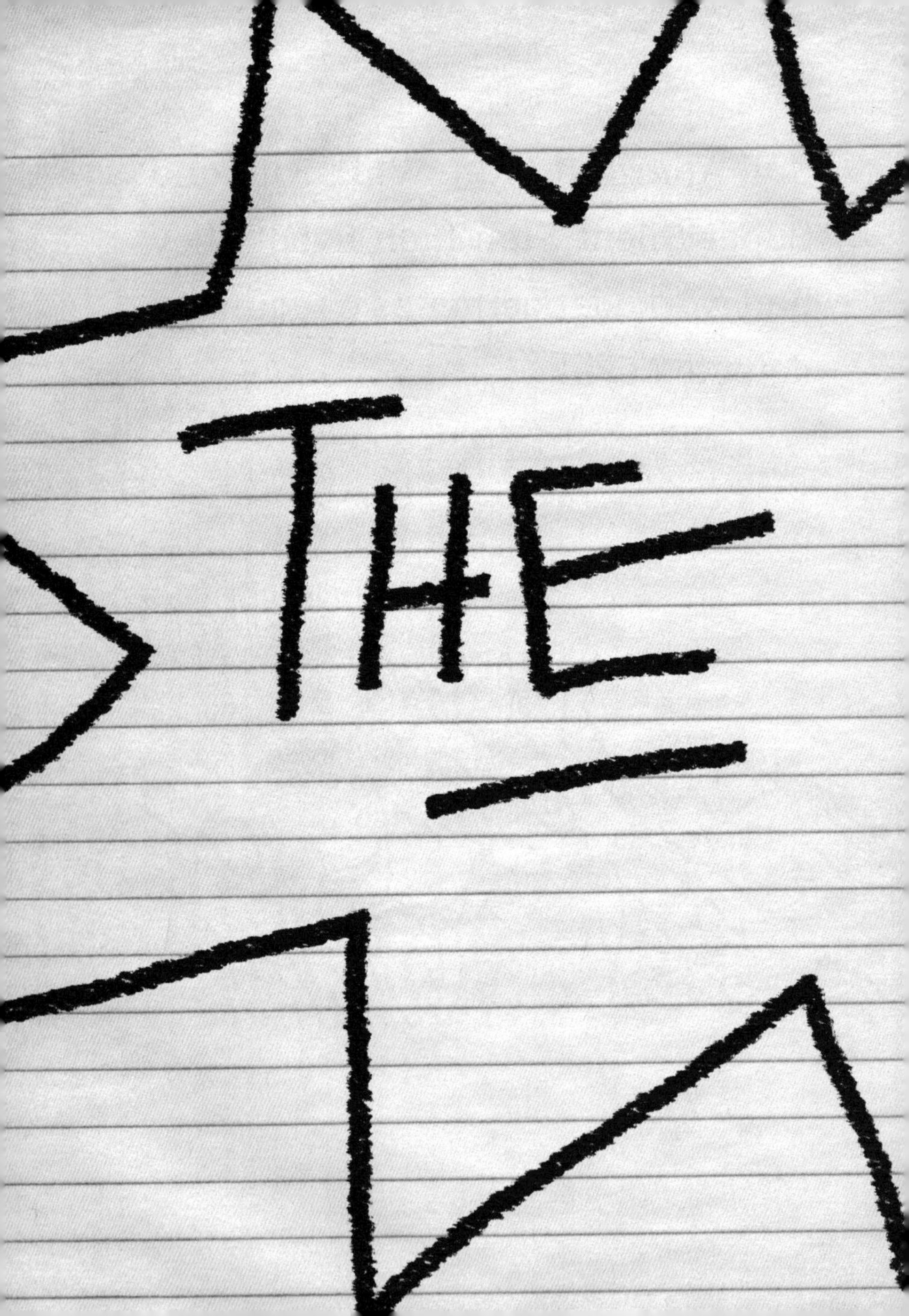
THE

END!

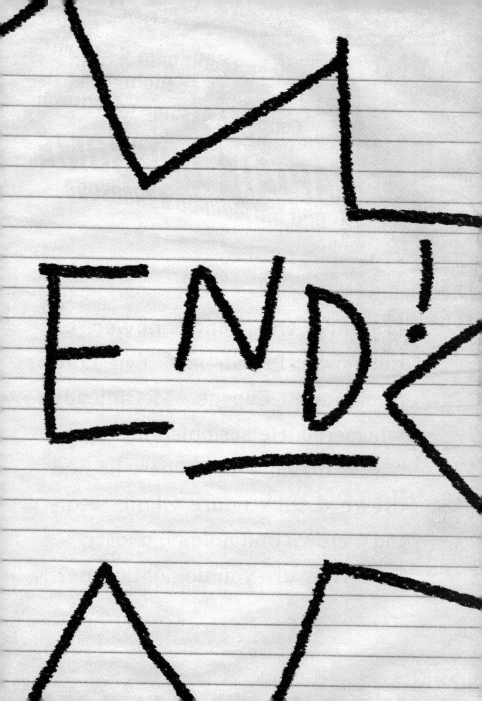

Keep reading for a sneak peek at the next Captain Awesome adventure!

CAPTAIN AWESOME
AND THE MUMMY'S TREASURE

Beware the pencil power of the Power Pencil,' says evil Lord Stickman!" Eugene McGillicudy whispered. He scribbled his pencil across his notebook where he had drawn a stick figure villain wearing a crown and holding a laser.

"How are you doing, Eugene?"

His best friend Charlie Thomas Jones held up his own drawing. It was a pile of liquid yellow cheese with red and blue spots. "Stick Figure Nacho Cheese Man just covered Stick Figure King Boulderface in hot pepper cheese," Charlie said. "I colored the cheese."

"What's with the blue spots?"

"My red marker dried out," Charlie explained. "So, who's going to defeat Lord Stickman?"

GALAXY ZACK

READING IS OUT OF THIS WORLD!